What's worse than a new stepfather? A week alone *with him!*

"Since I don't have to be back at work for a week," said Sally, "I thought it might be nice if Andrew and I took a little trip together . . . to really get to know each other. And then, Wedge, you can be alone here with King. We're going to have a whole lifetime together, so I think a week separated like that would be good for us. All of us."

Sally's voice trailed off in Wedge's mind, while his pancakes turned to rocks in his stomach. He thought he might cry if he wasn't careful. It was bad enough to have a pair of scarecrows for a new father and brother, but to be alone *with one of them for a week would be unbearable.*

"I can teach Wedge all about miniature golf—how to run a course. We'll have a great time. Right, son?"

Wonderful, Wedge thought. He rose from the table and ran to his room.

"Henkes's novelist's hand is as sure as his illustrative talents. A touching and funny book."   —*Publishers Weekly*

OTHER PUFFIN BOOKS YOU MAY ENJOY

TWO
UNDER
PAR

written and illustrated by
Kevin Henkes

PUFFIN BOOKS

PUFFIN BOOKS

Published by the Penguin Group

Penguin Books USA Inc., 375 Hudson Street, New York, New York 10014, U.S.A.

Penguin Books Ltd, 27 Wrights Lane, London W8 5TZ, England

Penguin Books Australia Ltd, Ringwood, Victoria, Australia

Penguin Books Canada Ltd, 10 Alcorn Avenue, Toronto, Ontario, Canada M4V 3B2

Penguin Books (N.Z.) Ltd, 182-190 Wairau Road, Auckland 10, New Zealand

Penguin Books Ltd, Registered Offices: Harmondsworth, Middlesex, England

First published in the United States of America by Greenwillow Books,
a division of William Morrow & Company, Inc., 1987
Reprinted by arrangement with William Morrow and Company, Inc.
Published in Puffin Books, 1997

1 3 5 7 9 10 8 6 4 2

LIBRARY OF CONGRESS CATALOGING-IN-PUBLICATION DATA

Henkes, Kevin.
Two under par / written and illustrated by Kevin Henkes.
p. cm.
Summary: When his mother's new marriage takes them into the household
of a miniature golf course owner, ten-year-old Wedge struggles with
feelings of resentment and dislike for his stepfather.
ISBN 0-14-038426-X (pbk.)
[1. Remarriage—Fiction. 2. Stepfathers—Fiction.] I. Title.
PZ7.H389Tw 1997 [Fic]—dc20 96-34912 CIP AC

Printed in the United States of America

For three of my favorite families, with love—
Henkes, Dronzek, Greenwillow

Contents

TO I-94

THE GROVE

THE HOUSE

THE SHED

HIGHWAY 5

TO DOWNTOWN

CAMELOT

MAYFIELD, WISCONSIN

1. The Scarecrows

The castle. Although it was only seven feet tall, it appeared oddly majestic with the sun rising in the east behind it. Its ornate spires glittered in the morning light, and the elongated shadows they cast ran across the tee-off mat, over the driveway, and pointed directly to Wedge's bedroom window like large arrows.

Wedge was sitting on his bed, his pajamas still on, rubbing the drowsiness from his puffy eyes. He yawned as he rose and shuffled across the rippling linoleum more like an old man than a ten-year-old boy. The floor creaked and groaned under his weight. He stopped at the window, squinting at the castle. Wedge scowled at the golden turrets. "I feel like I'm waking up in *Disneyland,*" he said to himself, disgusted.

It wasn't Disneyland. A far cry from it. Actually, it was King Arthur's Camelot—Mayfield, Wisconsin's first and only miniature golf course.

Arthur ("King") Simpson, Camelot's owner and Wedge's brand-new stepfather, had just opened the course at the end of the school year. Camelot was King's pride and joy. Wedge thought it was embarrassing. He couldn't understand why a grown man would pour his entire life into a miniature golf course, go by the nickname King, or parade around in public in a plastic gold crown with fake jewels glued on. *Especially* when he was married to your very own mother.

It didn't make any sense to Wedge. Sometimes nothing made sense to Wedge. In fact, *most of the time* nothing made sense to Wedge anymore.

For openers, Wedge never understood why his

real father had to take off before he was born and never come back. Wedge didn't even have a picture of him. And his mother's description of him—when Wedge pressed her for one—had a tendency to change from time to time. Drastically. Wedge wondered if she ever really got a good look at him.

Wedge also never understood why, out of the entire male population of Mayfield, his mother had to choose King for a husband. Two of Wedge's friends—Jackie DeRose and Eric Scheller—had stepfathers, too. But that was different. Wedge wasn't exactly sure *how* it was different, but he knew that it was. Maybe it had something to do with that stupid crown King always wore. (At least Jackie's stepdad had the decency to cover *his* head with a Milwaukee Brewers cap.) Or maybe it was because acquiring King was a package deal—along with him came his own son, Andrew.

Whenever Wedge looked at Andrew (who was five), he was reminded of King. And whenever he looked at King (who was thirty-eight), he was reminded of Andrew. In Wedge's opinion they both bordered on pathetic. They were thin and pale with lanky arms that hung down the sides of their bodies like long curtains. Their arms even moved like curtains would—floppy and smooth. And if the wind happened to be blowing, Wedge thought that they could pass for scarecrows— sleeves waving wildly about, as if they had no arms at all.

Their faces were almost white with pinkish splotches haphazardly cropping up here and there. The splotches turned deep red when King got angry or when Andrew was embarrassed. And their hair was like blond string, falling halfway down their faces in straight lines, partially covering their beaked noses. (Andrew's, incidentally, happened to be dripping quite frequently.)

Pitiful, Wedge thought. Extremely pitiful.

Wedge had physical problems of his own, but they were more tolerable; he looked almost normal. Most obvious was the fact that Wedge was slightly overweight. Possibly more than slightly overweight. Wedge liked to eat and it showed.

Wedge's other disability, only he, his mother, and his pediatrician knew about. The left side of his buttocks was completely covered with a large white spot. Doctor Harris said it was simply from a lack of pigment in his skin and that it was nothing to be alarmed about. The spot was in the shape of Texas, upside down.

Wedge vowed that no one else would ever see his spot, except for his wife if he ever got married. Which was highly unlikely because most of the girls he knew were like Judith Mills. And that was bad news.

Wedge was thinking that perhaps the spot meant that his real father was living in Texas somewhere, when his mother called from the hallway.

"Wedge! Andrew! Time for breakfast!"

"How can she sound so cheerful?" Wedge mumbled, taking one last look at the castle, before turning and heading for the good smells of the kitchen.

It didn't make sense.

Like everything else.

Nothing. Ever. Made. Sense.

*   *   *

When Wedge entered the kitchen, King and Andrew were already seated at the table eyeing stacks of steaming pancakes. Wedge could tell that King had done the cooking, because the pancakes were perfect, golden disks. Sally always made pancakes in the shapes of unidentifiable animals, which were usually broken, crumbled, or burned by the time they got to your plate. Wedge walked past his new father and brother without a word and sat at the far end of the table.

"Morning, Sally," Wedge said to his mother, who was waiting in her bright red robe by the stove for the teakettle to whistle. Her hair hung down past her shoulders, resembling spiral macaroni spray-painted bronze.

"Morning, honey," she replied with a toothy smile. Like a cardinal, she flitted around the table and pecked the top of his head, her robe swooshing about her.

For as long as he could remember, Wedge had always called his mother Sally. According to her, the terms mom, mother, and ma made her feel like an old lady. "Something I hope I never am," she said frequently.

"Does that mean you plan on dying young?" Wedge had asked once when he was in a temperamental mood and his mother's indignation at being called what she naturally was annoyed him. He even fleetingly pondered the possibility that she *wasn't* his mother, but quickly dismissed the thought.

"No," she had answered, "it just means that I plan on staying young in spirit until I'm at least one hundred."

"Please spare me the sight of seeing you in a bikini when you're over fifty, okay, Sally?" Wedge had said sarcastically, anger rising deep within him. But then, in a matter of minutes the anger had disappeared and he'd found himself surrounded by Sally's arms. Laughing. After all— until King and Andrew came along—they were all each other had. And, comparatively, Wedge had liked it that way.

Wedge's empty stomach growled during grace.

The noise was so loud that it took King and Andrew by surprise; Sally was used to it.

"How did you *do* that?" Andrew asked, pointing to Wedge's stomach and sniffling.

"Didn't your father ever tell you it was rude to point?" Wedge said, ignoring Andrew's question and pouring a large amount of maple syrup on his pancakes in a circular motion. His stomach growled again. "Excuse me," Wedge said, sneering at Andrew.

The teakettle whistled. Sally fixed herself a cup of almond tea (without sugar) and sat down at the table next to King. Besides the tea, all Sally had for breakfast was half a grapefruit. She wasn't even slightly overweight (more like downright skinny)—but she watched her diet carefully, keeping track of her daily calorie intake. "I'm *so* fat," she'd often say as she looked in the bathroom mirror or passed a storefront window.

In Wedge's opinion, Sally's concern with her weight was like Rapunzel complaining that her hair was too short. Enough to drive you nuts. But she rarely commented on his own weight or monitored his food drastically, which he appreciated.

Sally sighed loudly, getting everyone's attention. She drew in another long breath and gently pushed her teacup away from herself. "I came up with a real winner of an idea this morning," she began, toying with one of her curls, her lips slowly curving up in a smile.

"What is it, Sal?" King asked.

"Well, it concerns all of us. And I think it's real important. Especially because two families of two have become one family of four. . . ."

I wish she'd get to the point, Wedge thought. He had taken a piece of bread from the bread box on the counter and was using it to soak up the syrup that was left on his plate. He was paying more attention to his sticky creation than to his mother, but when she finally announced what she had been working up to, he heard every horrible word.

"Since I don't have to be back to work for a week, I thought it might be nice if Andrew and I took a little trip together—to the Dells or to Madison or somewhere—to really get to know each other. And then, Wedge, you can be alone here with King. We're going to have a whole lifetime together, so I think a week separated like that would be good for us. All of us."

Sally's voice trailed off in Wedge's mind, while his pancakes turned to rocks in his stomach. He thought he might cry if he wasn't careful. It was bad enough to have a pair of scarecrows for a new father and brother, but to be *alone* with one of them for a week would be unbearable.

"Could we go camping, Sally?" Andrew asked, twirling his fork in delight.

"Sure, sweetie," Sally answered. "Well, Wedge, King—what do you think?"

"That's what I call a short honeymoon," King said, laughing. "But I can teach Wedge all about miniature golf—how to run a course. We'll have a great time. Right, son?"

Wonderful, Wedge thought. He rose from the table and ran to his room. He was speechless. Speechless because he didn't know what to say. And because he was afraid that if he opened his mouth, nothing but a sob would come out.

2. The Box

Wedge locked his bedroom door (thank goodness he didn't have to share his room with Andrew) and lay on his bed, his head buried beneath his pillow. "I'm not going to cry," he repeated over and over to himself. "I'm not going to cry." But it did no good. And once the tears started they flowed free and easy. If body size has anything to do with the amount of tears a person has stored inside, I'll be here forever, Wedge thought absently. Maybe I'll even drown.

His drifting thoughts of self-pity were interrupted by a brisk knocking on the door. "Wedge? Open up, honey. Come on, Wedge. Let's talk. Please?" Sally's voice coaxed.

Part of him wanted to ignore Sally—leave her behind the locked door along with her stupid idea—but a larger part of him needed her. Needed her now. Wedge walked to the door, wiping a few tears aside on the way. "Wedge," she said, motioning with her arms for him to be hugged when he opened the door. "Oh, Wedge."

They worked their way over to Wedge's bed. Sally pushed his hair out of his eyes and rocked him—back and forth, back and forth—as best she could. She hadn't done this in years, and she knew she couldn't do it very long, considering Wedge's weight and her slender frame.

"I just can't be here with *him*. For a *week*. *Alone.*" Wedge's voice was squeaking. "I just can't. Don't make me, Sally."

"Wedge, honey, his name is King and he's your father now," Sally said gently. "You've finally got the one thing you've always wanted."

"I want my *real* dad."

"Oh, Wedge, let's not start this again. We've gone over it too many times already. You've never really *had* a father—and now you do. And King loves you and wants you to love him back. Let's be happy. It'll be okay. I promise." Sally turned Wedge's face, their eyes meeting. "I promise," she reassured. "And a promise is a promise."

Wedge's tears stopped, but he didn't feel any better.

"I know everything happened so fast—me getting married, moving out here away from the apartment, and you getting a new father and brother. It's a lot."

That's an understatement, Wedge thought, his sadness turning to anger.

"But think of Andrew—it's the same thing for him," Sally said. "He's got you and me for a new brother and mother. And he never knew his real mother, either—she died when he was born."

"I know," Wedge said, thinking that that was all beside the point.

Sally explained once more how important she thought the trip was for all of them. She was trying too hard to be cheerful and Wedge sensed it. "And you two will have a lot of fun together. King's real funny."

That's the problem, Wedge thought—he's embarrassing. Wedge suddenly felt bold. "Why did you have to go and get married, anyway?" he asked. Bolder and bolder. "You hardly even *know* him."

"That's enough, Wedge," Sally said, flustered. She flipped her coppery hair over her shoulder as she got up off the bed. "Let's talk happy." She turned and looked at Wedge once more, her big, brown eyes glistening now. "I *really* want to make this work."

The way she looked at him—her eyes about to tear—gave Wedge the chills. He'd have jumped off Gunther's Bridge or gone without eating for a month if she'd have asked him to right then.

"Okay, Sally."

"That's my Wedge."

Wedge watched Sally slowly walk out into the

tea-colored light of the hallway. She blew him a kiss and forced a smile.

"Okay, Mom," he whispered to her back.

Most of Wedge's belongings were still packed, the boxes stacked in crooked rows along the walls of his room and in his closet. Wedge pushed open the drape that covered the closet and pulled out a box the size of a small portable TV. He carried the box to his bed. Before he opened the box he locked the bedroom door again and pulled the window shade down. The room became dark and fuzzy.

The box and its contents were a secret—not even Sally knew about them. Hidden beneath the cardboard flaps were things Wedge had bought or collected. Things he would give his real father if he ever came home. Things Wedge could bring to him when Wedge was old enough to drive and could look for him.

Wedge fingered the objects. There was a set of miniature screwdrivers, a bottle of after-shave, and a pair of plastic pens that were covered in brown paper to make them look as if they were made of

wood. Wedge had purchased these gifts at Jeffer-
son Elementary. Every year before Christmas vacation, each class was separately taken to the gym,
which was decorated like the North Pole. Some of
the mothers and teachers' aides were dressed like
elves. They sold small Christmas gifts at prices
kids could afford—the proceeds going to build a
new art room. Santa's Secret Shop, they called it.
The first year they had it, some mother Wedge
didn't recognize showed him the set of miniature
screwdrivers. She wore a hat with a little bell that
jingled as she talked.

"I bet your father would love this," she said,
smiling and jingling. "And it's only ninety-five
cents."

A lump rose in Wedge's throat. He didn't want
to explain to the lady that he didn't even know
what his father looked like. "Yeah," he said
slowly. "I'll take it."

That night, at home, he put the screwdrivers in
a box and hid the box under his bed. Gradually he
started adding to the box. These are gifts for my
dad, Wedge thought. Gifts to show him how

much I love him. Gifts to give him whenever he decides to come home. *If* he ever decides to come home.

Other things in the box included a baseball Wedge had found in the empty lot behind his old apartment building, on which he forged Robin Yount's autograph, and a complete set of his Sears pixie-pinups and school pictures he had recently taken out of Sally's photo album.

Wedge was putting the photos in chronological order, trying to pinpoint exactly when he started gaining weight, when he heard what sounded like a cat scratching at the door.

"Who's there?" he called, quickly tossing the photos back in the box, closing the flaps, and shoving it under his bed.

More scratching. And then a thin, mosquito voice that said: "Wedge? It's Andrew. You gonna come out?"

"Why?" Wedge asked. What do you care, anyway, you droopy little snotnose? he said to himself.

"Sally and Dad want all of us to play a game of

golf together. Before Sally takes me camping." He
kept scratching at the door and trying to turn the
knob. "Come on, Wedge. Afraid I'll beat ya?"

Wedge, still in his pajamas, sprang from his
bed. "We'll see who beats who, Androop," he
said, pulling Andrew down the hallway behind
him.

Wedge didn't beat Andrew. Wedge didn't beat
anyone. He lost his temper on the third hole and
quit. "This is a stupid game," he complained,
tossing his putter in the grass and walking away.

Wedge sat on the porch while King, Sally, and
Andrew finished playing. He stayed there for
more than an hour. Sulking. Pretending to ignore
Sally as she packed the Volkswagen.

When Sally and Andrew were ready to go, Sally
hugged Wedge and placed a note in his hand. It
said: *I love you, Wedge. Thanks for helping me make
this work. I'll call you every night—I promise. And a
promise is a promise. Love, Sally.* It was written in
Sally's familiar, loopy penmanship. Wedge crumbled the note, but placed it in his pajama pocket.

"Bye, Wedge! Bye, King!" Sally called a dozen times. "Bye, guys!"

King was waving goodbye so fast and hard his arm reminded Wedge of a windshield wiper.

"Bye, Dad! Bye, Wedge!" Andrew chirped. He wiped his nose on his sleeve before climbing into the car.

"Hey, Androop, don't you know what tissues are for?!" Wedge yelled from the porch. Without waving, Wedge watched the Beetle disappear down the long driveway.

Sally and Andrew were on their way.

And Wedge was alone with King.

3. Judith Mills

King Simpson's Camelot was open to the public each morning at eleven o'clock. Sally and Andrew had pulled away at approximately ten-thirty. So after Wedge washed and dressed, he had about twenty minutes to walk around the course before any customers might arrive.

King had asked Wedge to help him prepare for the day's golfers. "I'll teach you the ropes of the business, Wedge. You can wear my crown, and I'll even let you work the cash register."

"No, thanks," Wedge had replied, a hint of a snarl in his voice. "I think I was born with a low energy quotient, anyway."

"Maybe later, then?"

"I doubt it."

"Have it your way," King had said, the pink splotches on his face darkening.

Wedge pretended he hated Camelot, but drifting around from hole to hole—surrounded by the castle on the eighteenth hole, knights with mechanical arms on the fifteenth, a dragon on the seventh whose spiked tail slowly rose and dropped blocking the cup, and the large silver swords that marked each tee-off mat—Wedge found himself fascinated. Drawn to it because metal knights were more noble than a particular stepfather. And a seven-foot castle more appealing than a new place to live. Especially when the new place was on the outskirts of town, miles away from your friends and from where you've lived your whole life.

Wedge circled the course twice, then sat by the side of the house, resting against the brick foundation. The sun was high and hot. Wedge closed his eyes and raised his head to the heat. It felt good as it soaked in.

The house had gray shingled walls and stood two stories tall. Between it and the course King had built a shed that served as storage for the putters and multicolored golf balls used on the course. It also housed the old cash register and the electrical switches that turned on and off the knights and the dragon, and controlled the large overhead lights used at night.

King was sweeping the sidewalk that led from the shed to the first tee. His thin fingers were like spider legs clinging to the broom handle. And his crown gleamed when the sun caught it a certain way. Wedge watched him and daydreamed. He wished he was someplace else. Anywhere.

The house, the shed, and the miniature golf course were nestled between two tiny groves, about a mile off Interstate 94 on Highway S. There was a McDonald's just another mile down the road; because of that, most of King's customers were families who got talked into a game of miniature golf by their children on their way back to I-94 after eating. It was the middle of summer, and business was good.

The sun grew hotter, so Wedge—wet with sweat—moved around to the shady backside of the house. He lay down on the soft grass, remembering the winter night, years earlier, when Sally had read him a story (he couldn't recall the title) about a knight who slayed a fire-breathing dragon. The pictures in the book were brightly colored— the dragon was blackish green and the fire that roared from his mouth was red and blue and orange. The paintings of the dragon scared Wedge back then, but he liked the feeling. Long after Sally had turned out the light and left his room, Wedge kept opening the book, stealing a peek at the dragon, and slamming the book closed in horror. The dragon seemed to move off the pages in the shadowy night.

Sally worked at the Mayfield Library, checking out books and shelving them. She often brought home picture books to read aloud to Wedge at bedtime. As he got older, the books got longer.

Real chapter books that took weeks to finish and had to be renewed. *Winnie the Pooh. Charlotte's Web. The Wind in the Willows.*

"I want you to know the classics, Wedge," Sally had said once, before she began reading. "I never read them until I worked at the library. You'll be getting a real head start. At least you'll know a lot more than I did at your age."

Camelot reminded Wedge of that picture book again—that knight and that dragon. He envisioned them coming to life—the dragon turning King into a pile of ashes that the wind would blow away.

But like a circle, Wedge's mind always ended up where it started. Thinking about Sally. And missing her.

Just then Wedge's stomach rumbled—it was time for a snack.

After preparing a peanut-butter-and-cream-cheese sandwich, Wedge poured himself a glass of milk and sat down at the kitchen table. While he ate, he watched the golfers who were making their way around the course. One golfer in particular caught his eye—she looked just like Judith Mills, except that her hair wasn't black enough.

Judith, along with Jackie DeRose and Eric Scheller, were Wedge's friends from the apartment building he used to call home. Sometimes Judith seemed more like an enemy than a friend, but Wedge missed not having her right across the hall.

Besides sending Wedge notes with hearts drawn all over them, Judith was the one who thought of the nickname Wedge.

"You look like a wedge," she said to him one day at lunch, when they were in the second grade. That morning in science class they had learned about pulleys, wedges, ropes, and wheels. "You've got a small head and you just keep getting wider all the way down," she observed. Then she made kissing sounds and stuck her tongue out at him.

From that day on everyone called him Wedge —even Sally and his teachers. Wedge never thought the nickname actually fit—*he* didn't think he looked anything like a wedge—but he liked it much better than his real name. His real

name was Conrad (after a character on Sally's favorite soap opera).

Wedge finished his sandwich. He decided to
call Judith on the phone. Maybe, he thought, Judith's mother could drive her, Jackie, and Eric out
to play miniature golf. He smiled as he dialed the
number. He felt better than he had all morning.

"Hellome?" Judith's familiar voice said.

"Judith, this is Wedge."

"Wedge? Wedge who?" she asked, giggling.

"Come on, you know."

More giggling.

"I miss you," Wedge said suddenly. He didn't
know why he said it—he hadn't planned on it. It
just came out.

The giggling stopped.

"I didn't want to move," Wedge added. "I
wish I could move back."

"You know," Judith said in a serious voice,
"my mom said the only reason Sally got married
and you moved away is because she's pregnant. In
case you don't know—that means she's having a
baby and—"

Wedge dropped the phone. Then he picked it up and hung it up without saying another word to Judith. He felt weak. He began to tremble.

Of course he knew what pregnant meant. As a matter of fact, it was Judith who had told him.

Wedge dialed Judith's number again.

"Hellome?" It was Judith.

"You stink worse than a wet dog!" Wedge shouted. He slammed down the receiver, his heart pounding as if it might jump right out of his body.

It was still pounding as fast and hard ten minutes later.

4. Aunt Bonnie and Uncle Larry

Wedge dialed another number (his heart still drumming) and listened to the phone ring. "Please answer," he whispered into the receiver. The phone kept ringing. And ringing.

"Hello?" an out-of-breath voice finally said.

Wedge sighed in relief. "Aunt Bonnie? This is Wedge."

"Oh, hi, honey. How are you?"

"I'm okay," he lied. "Are you going to be home for a while?"

"I sure am. Your Uncle Larry and I are working in the garden. And we've got enough weeds to keep us occupied all afternoon."

"Mind if I come over?"

"You know you're always welcome, honey."

Wedge forgot to say thank you and goodbye. He darted from the kitchen and snuck his bike out of the basement. He headed in the direction of Aunt Bonnie and Uncle Larry's house. He didn't tell King he was going.

The one and only good thing about moving in with King was that now Wedge lived less than a mile from Aunt Bonnie and Uncle Larry. Just a short bike ride away.

Wedge loved Aunt Bonnie and Uncle Larry's house more than anyplace on earth. It smelled sweet and spicy like gingersnaps, and their thick sofa and chairs were the kind that settled in around you when you sat—making getting out of them as hard as rising from a warm bed on a cold morning. The walls were light and airy, the floors deep dark chocolate shag. Outside—flowers and shrubs surrounded the house in bright clusters.

Wedge pedaled furiously. He was forming questions in his mind to ask his aunt. Questions about Sally. He wondered if he should come right out and say, "Is Sally having a baby?" But he didn't think he could actually say those words, and he knew how miserable he'd be if he heard a certain answer. He decided to simply bring up the topic of babies and see where it led.

For a moment Wedge convinced himself that it was all a joke. It would be just like Judith to kid around like that, Wedge thought as he jumped the curb and veered into Aunt Bonnie's backyard. But the terrible gnawing in his stomach (it wasn't hunger) didn't go away. And stomachs never lie.

"Wedge!" Aunt Bonnie called. "Come give me a hug and a kiss."

Wedge dropped his bike on the wide, sloping lawn and ran toward her. "Hi!" he said.

Aunt Bonnie was wearing denim coveralls and she carried a forked digging tool that looked like a snake's tongue in her gloved hand. When she smiled, her teeth showed just the way Sally's did, and her eyes had the same sparkle. But the sim-

ilarities between Sally and Bonnie ended there—
not much for sisters to have in common.

Bonnie was taller and heavier. Her hair was
lighter and her voice deeper. Details were important to Bonnie; Sally didn't let details bother her.
For example, in Wedge's first year of Cub Scouts,
instead of sewing his cloth insignias on his uni-
form (like everyone else), Sally glued them on
with Elmer's to save time. "No one'll know the
difference, honey," she told Wedge. But Bonnie
noticed. So she offered to stitch them on. And she
did, with all the precision of an accomplished
seamstress. Aunt Bonnie kept a spotless house;
Sally didn't believe in dusting or vacuuming except in emergencies. Sometimes Wedge thought
that Sally and Aunt Bonnie were as different as
two sisters could be. Like vinegar and oil in a
salad dressing that just won't stay mixed long,
even though they belong together.

While Wedge wriggled away from Aunt Bonnie's hug, Uncle Larry came out of the garage.
The expression on his face was frequently that of a
young child who had just done something he

shouldn't have. "Hi, Wedge-O!" he yelled. He wiped his right hand on his jeans and outstretched it for Wedge to shake.

"Hi, Uncle Larry," Wedge said, cringing from Larry's firm grip. Uncle Larry used to be a football star at Mayfield High. He even played a season with the Badgers before he dropped out of college. His hands were the size of Wedge's baseball mitt (the rest of his body was in relative proportion), making his handshake deadly.

Once, Wedge put his hands in his pockets and kept them there to avoid his uncle's famous grasp. But that was worse—Uncle Larry got down in a three-point stance and charged after Wedge. He picked Wedge up, tossed him in the air a few times, and then ran around the yard pretending Wedge was a football. It had happened after dinner, and consequently Wedge lost his stuffed porkchops all over Aunt Bonnie's purple rhododendrons.

"What brings you here?" Uncle Larry asked, as Wedge blew on his hand and tried to wiggle some life back into it.

"Um." Wedge didn't know what to say. "Just to say hi, I guess."

"How's your new family? And your new house?" Aunt Bonnie asked. "Come sit by the picnic table and fill us in."

"Well, one thing's certain," Uncle Larry said, lightly jabbing Wedge's stomach. "It looks like your new dad's been feeding you okay." Aunt Bonnie shot Uncle Larry a disgusted look, but Wedge didn't care. He never minded when Uncle Larry teased him. A few jokes and his handshakes were well worth suffering through. After all, Uncle Larry made the best fudge walnut brownies Wedge had ever tasted, and he regularly took Wedge to Brewers and Bucks games.

Wedge told them all about Sally and Andrew's trip and how he was stuck in a new house with a scarecrow who wore a crown.

Uncle Larry rested his arm on Wedge's shoulder and chuckled. "Come on, Wedge-O, it can't be that bad. It'll just take some getting used to. King seems like a nice guy, and it must be great fun to have a miniature golf course in your own backyard."

"Not really."

"Why don't you stay here for a few hours," Aunt Bonnie suggested pleasantly. "We can have lunch outside. We'll have a good time together, and then we can put your bike in the pickup and drive you home in plenty of time for dinner."

"I wish I could stay with you tonight," Wedge said. "Maybe even *live* with you."

"Now, Wedge," Aunt Bonnie said, a worried look on her face, "you're the most important person in Sally's life. Always were, always will be. Without you she just wouldn't function. And I'm sure King would be brokenhearted if you slept here tonight. Furthermore—I think the four of you make a handsome family."

Speaking of families, it seemed like a big waste to Wedge that Aunt Bonnie and Uncle Larry didn't have kids. They'd be perfect parents. That thought brought Wedge's mind back to his phone call with Judith. And to babies. Mustering all the courage he could, Wedge asked, "Why don't you guys have kids? You know, a baby."

The second the words came out of his mouth, he regretted them.

Aunt Bonnie blushed instantly, matching the color of her pink geraniums. "Oh . . . Wedge," she stammered. "Well, Wedge, some people just have kids . . ."

"And some don't," Uncle Larry added quickly, in a stern yet gentle tone that indicated that the subject was off limits as far as he was concerned. He winked at Wedge. "Come on, team, we've got a slew of weeds to annihilate."

As he walked to the garage to get a small shovel, Wedge wondered if Aunt Bonnie and Uncle Larry always seemed so happy together because they *didn't* have kids. Maybe it was kids who caused all the trouble. And maybe, he thought, my real father left because I was on the way. Wedge decided that if Sally was really having a baby, he'd take off, too. For good.

They spent the afternoon working in the garden, only taking a break for lunch. Then Uncle

Larry and Wedge made brownies while Aunt Bonnie arranged vases of her prized flowers throughout the house. While they waited for the brownies to come out of the oven, Wedge wished that he had the power to stop time. If he could, he'd have stopped it right then and stayed there forever.

5. Eavesdropping

Wedge, Aunt Bonnie, and Uncle Larry were back outdoors—sitting in lawn chairs by the flower bed in the side yard—when King pulled up in front of the house. The car screeched to a lurching halt. Wedge spotted the large, gold, fancy letters that spelled Camelot across the car doors instantly. His heart sank.

King dashed up the sidewalk and across the grass. "Wedge! There you are!" he said loudly.

"Thank God." He sighed deeply in relief and patted Wedge's head.

Wedge shrank away from King. Patting heads, Wedge thought, is something you do to dogs and cats. Not people.

"I was worried about you," King explained. He was talking fast and puffing. "You should have told me where you were going."

Wedge shrugged his shoulders and absently scratched a mosquito bite. "Oh," was all he managed to say. He was staring at the ground, shifting his feet.

King slowed down a bit and said hello to Aunt Bonnie and Uncle Larry. Then he told his story. About how he had discovered Wedge was missing. About how he had looked everywhere for him. At Sally and Wedge's old apartment building, the arcade in downtown Mayfield, the library, the department store, the playground, the public pool, the riverbank, Gunther's Bridge, McDonald's. Then he had telephoned everyone he could think of; no one knew where Wedge was. He had even called Bonnie and Larry, but nobody had answered. So he made the rounds of town again. And again.

Aunt Bonnie kept apologizing; she had heard the phone ring, but was tired of running in from the garden, wiping her feet, and racing through the house to get to the phone. "If only I'd answered that phone . . ." she said. "I'm so sorry."

"And *I'm* sorry you had to worry, King," Uncle Larry added. "I just assumed Wedge told you he was with us."

"Don't apologize," King said. Suddenly he didn't know what to do with his hands. He started jingling his keys. "I'm just glad I thought of checking here on my way home."

Wedge felt squirmy—he hated being talked about—so he crouched as low as he could in the garden, making himself as small as possible, and began digging enthusiastically.

Aunt Bonnie got up and motioned toward the house with a graceful sweep of her arm. "Come inside and sit down, King. I'll make a pitcher of iced tea." She led the way around the house to the back door. "I hope you like brownies!" she called.

Wedge grabbed four brownies off the tray that Aunt Bonnie had prepared. On the tray were three glasses, three spoons, three napkins, a pitcher of iced tea, sugar, lemon slices, and a plate heaped with fat brownies. There had been four glasses, four spoons, and four napkins on the tray, but Wedge had taken off one of each and set them back on the counter.

"Now, Wedge, you're *sure* you don't want to sit in the living room with us?" Aunt Bonnie asked for the second time.

"I'm sure."

"Stuffy adults?"

"Something like that." Wedge headed for the back door. "I'm going to mess around outside!" he yelled from the hallway. He opened and slammed the back door—making it sound as though he had gone out. He waited, silently counting to one hundred. Then he tiptoed back into the kitchen. He crept along the wall and knelt down by the sink. Craning his head around the doorframe, he kept as quiet as he knew how. He had a sneaking suspicion he was going to be talked about again. And even though he hated that thought, his curiosity won out. He stayed. And hid. And watched. And listened.

Wedge could see the backs of King's and Uncle Larry's heads. They appeared to be sinking into the deep sofa. Swallowed by its softness. Aunt Bonnie was sitting in the rocking chair. Wedge couldn't see her, but he could hear the chair creak, then moan, creak, then moan.

Iced tea was poured. Ice cubes clattered. And the talking began.

"I'm counting on your being hungry," Wedge heard Aunt Bonnie say.

King said, "Thank you," and "Your garden is beautiful."

Now it was Aunt Bonnie and Uncle Larry's turn to say thank you.

They talked about Uncle Larry's being laid off from the canning plant and his part-time job at K Mart. They talked about the Blombergs' dog, Patsy, who got heatstroke. Then it got interesting.

"Where's Wedge?" King asked.

Wedge's ears perked up.

"He's outside," Aunt Bonnie answered. Creak, then moan, creak, then moan, went the chair.

There was a silence before King said to Uncle

Larry, "Sally's told me you've been like a father to Wedge. Taking him places. To ball games."

"Oh, I guess I just try to help him out when he needs it. Fill some of the holes in his life."

Wedge sucked in his breath. He was afraid to listen. Afraid not to.

King again: "I don't know what to do or say to Wedge. I really want him to like me—but it looks like that'll be easier said than done. And it's hard when they're not your own—you have to be so delicate. Any tips? You two seem to know him so well."

"I think time will do it," Aunt Bonnie said.

"Yeah," Uncle Larry agreed. "Just hang in there, King. Wedge is a good kid. A *big* one," he added, chuckling. "But seriously, I think he's got a big heart, too. It's just hidden under a few too many pounds of loneliness and confusion." A pause. "I always told Bonnie I didn't envy the man who might eventually marry Sally, because he'd have his hands full with Wedge. And with the trouble he's always had dealing with not having a father." Another pause. "You know, he scared off two men from the Big Brothers organization in record time. One afternoon was too much for both of them."

"*Larry,*" Aunt Bonnie said in a tone that meant: *Please be quiet.* Wedge could picture her disgusted look.

But Uncle Larry went on. "For a while he told the kids at school that his father was an Arctic explorer. Then it was a high-wire performer in France, or something. Last I heard, it was an oil tycoon in Dallas. You can't really blame him, though—sometimes dreaming gets you through a rough day. Or a rough night."

Wedge had heard enough. Eavesdropping wasn't all it was cracked up to be. It was a different kind of hurt, but it was more painful than the dentist's drill. He felt dull. His head was hazy. At first he thought he'd go outside as he had pretended to. But he knew they'd just keep talking about him. And that would be just as bad as (if not worse than) hearing every uncomfortable word. Because then he'd end up imagining what they were saying.

Wedge knew one way to end their talking. He simply waltzed in on them as if nothing had happened and caught them by surprise. "I ran out of brownies," he announced.

Aunt Bonnie turned with a start. "Oh! Wedge!"

Uncle Larry stuffed a whole brownie into his mouth, then loudly smacked his lips like a popgun going off.

And King started muttering. "Uh. The garden is *really* beautiful."

"Thank you," Aunt Bonnie replied. Wedge felt as if he were on "The Twilight Zone." As if he had been here before. Mr. Saunders, his science teacher from last year, called it déjà-vu. "But we're fighting a losing battle with our weeds," Aunt Bonnie continued. "They're definitely strong willed."

They all laughed. Except Wedge. He was thinking of *his* losing battle.

Because Wedge was there, they only talked about polite things now—grocery prices, the weather, lawn care. And that was perfectly fine with Wedge. He hung onto the adults the way a barnacle does to a boat—never letting them out of his sight or his hearing range.

King and Wedge stayed for dinner. Wedge was on his best behavior. Afterward, Uncle Larry brought out dusty old photo albums and they looked at Sally's and Bonnie's baby pictures. Baby pictures, Wedge thought, are the last thing I want to see.

"We better get going!" Wedge said suddenly, rising from the depths of the sofa, remembering his note. "Sally's going to call me! She told me she would! She could be trying right now!"

King put Wedge's bike in the trunk. Aunt Bonnie and Uncle Larry waved good night.

"The day turned out okay after all," King said to Wedge in an optimistic voice.

"Says who?" Wedge whispered back. Wedge swallowed hard as he got into the car. It seemed small and dark and like a prison. He was dreading this night more than he had ever dreaded anything in his entire life.

6. Sally's Call

Silence filled the car, barely leaving enough room for its two passengers. Wedge didn't feel like talking. King was at a loss for words. As they drove the short distance through the growing darkness, the day's events played back in Wedge's head like a broken record. Over and over. This was definitely one of his worst days. Ever. And the fact that it was almost night didn't help things.

There was something about nighttime that

Wedge didn't like. He wasn't afraid of monsters hiding in the shadows or ghosts watching from around corners, anymore. But he was less sure of himself at night. His confidence faded with the light.

It was after ten o'clock. Wedge had been waiting by the upstairs extension phone ever since he and King had arrived home. All the while he waited, he held the note Sally had written him. It smelled of lilacs. Just like Sally. It was the perfume she always wore. Sometimes she sprayed it on so generously that Wedge referred to her as "The Walking Perfume Factory" or "The Human Lilac Bush," and it made him feel queasy, especially if they were in the Volkswagen with the windows rolled up. But that night he continued to sniff the note even though the scent of lilacs had already made him feel light-headed.

The phone finally rang. Wedge answered it before the first ring was even completed.

"Sally?!"

"Will you accept a collect call from a Sally?" someone asked, sounding distant and formal.

"Yes!" Wedge cried. "Sally?!"

"Wedge! Hi, baby!" Wedge listened carefully to Sally's voice. The sound of every word. "How are you?"

Loaded question, Wedge thought. Not knowing where to start. What to say.

"Wedge? Are you there?"

"Yeah. And, uh, I wish you were here, too." His throat tightened. "You think you might come home *early*?"

At that point King picked up the phone in the kitchen. "Sal? Is that you?"

"Hi, King," Sally said. "Do you care if I talk to Wedge alone for a few minutes? Then Andrew and I will tell you all about our day." Sally made a kissing sound, the phone clicked, and King was gone.

"Wedge," Sally began, "remember our talk this morning? Let's be happy. I know everything's been a big rush, but I want to get to know the *real* Andrew and I want King to get to know the *real* you. This seemed like the best way. It really did. And you know me, Wedge, sometimes I just *do* things."

I think I know what else you did, Wedge thought. He found himself feeling angry, too, now. Lonely and angry.

Sally continued. "It's like jumping off the high dive at the public pool. You can sit around and wait and get yourself all worked up and scared. Or you can take a deep breath, close your eyes, and *jump!* I like to jump. Do you know what I mean, honey?"

Maybe you jump too often, Wedge said in his head.

"Honey?"

Wedge hated the high dive. Whenever he climbed up the ladder to the board, he saw double and the way the board swayed when he stood on it made his ears pound with blood. But if you didn't go through with it and jump, everyone laughed at you. Wedge also hated the high dive because he hated swimming. And he hated swimming because he didn't like to wear a swimming suit. He even disliked short pants. They made him feel uncomfortable and nervous. Fatter. No matter how hot it was, long pants were the only way to go.

But if given the choice, he'd rather be perched atop the high dive completely naked than be where he was at this moment.

"Wedge? *Wedge?*" Sally called, bringing his attention back to their conversation.

Wedge didn't answer, though. Words dangled in his throat, but he couldn't squeeze them out. If he wasn't able to see Sally for a week he didn't think he wanted to talk to her, either. It was too hard. It just made things worse. And anyway, what was he supposed to say?

"Wedge? Is this a bad connection?"

"It must be," he replied, making his voice crackle and thumping the phone with his thumb. "I'll tell King to come back on."

Wedge placed the receiver on the floor and yelled downstairs to King.

"I love you, Wedge!" Sally shouted into the phone.

Wedge stared at the receiver. He stared and stared. Against his better judgment, he decided to give eavesdropping one more try. So, instead of placing the receiver back in its cradle to give King and Sally their privacy, Wedge lay down on the floor, inching his ear up to it.

Sally was talking. ". . . and if things are that bad, I'll come home right now. I will."

"No. Really," King replied. "I want to do this on my own."

"Are you sure?"

"I'm sure."

"*Really?*"

"Really."

"Was this a bad idea?" Sally asked, sounding apologetic.

Wedge didn't quite understand King's reply. "Well," he said, "it was great in theory."

Then they both laughed. A happy-sad-exhausted laugh.

Sally said that they were staying in Madison. The next day they'd be visiting the capitol and the zoo. Then they'd go camping. Andrew was being a real gentleman, she told King. A real little trooper. Next, Andrew came on the line sounding like an overexcited mouse with the sniffles. Then

Sally and King whispered how much they loved and missed each other.

Wedge couldn't stand to listen any longer. He left the phone on the floor and went to his room, the note still pressed in the palm of his hand. He changed into his pajamas and plopped down in bed. He didn't know what to think. He curled tightly around his pillow. Hugging with all his might. Falling asleep easily would be nearly impossible. He kept smelling lilacs and hearing Sally's words: *". . . and if things are that bad, I'll come home right now."*

Wedge was starting to get an idea. Working out the details would get him through the long, lonely night.

7. Wedge's Idea

It was still dark when Wedge woke up. He had been dreaming. Dreaming about Sally's wedding. In reality, it had been a small ceremony at the courthouse in downtown Mayfield just two days earlier. No one came because that was the way Sally had wanted it. It had been only the four of them—Sally, King, Wedge, and Andrew. But in Wedge's dream it was different.

In his dream, Judith, Jackie, and Eric were there. The rest of Wedge's classmates were there, too. And so was a big, tall man wearing a black three-piece suit, a black cowboy hat, and mirror sunglasses. Wedge knew that the man was his real father. He had to be.

When the judge got to the part about vesting his power and pronouncing King and Sally man and wife, the cowboy jumped up, grabbed Sally, kissed her, took Wedge by the hand, and whisked them out of the courthouse. Outside, a silver limousine with Texas longhorns as a hood ornament was waiting. The three of them happily sped away, while Wedge's classmates cheered and King and Andrew stood with their mouths dropped open like big *O*'s.

Wedge had added the part about the limo after he woke up, but it was a good dream just the same. One of his best.

Wedge glanced at the Big Ben alarm clock on his dresser. Its small, round face glowed, so you could read it easily no matter what time it was. Three forty-five A.M. the clock indicated. Wedge knew he couldn't fall asleep again. He stared upward, remembering the dream and adding more details to it. The ceiling could have been the night sky, it was still so dark. Wedge was thinking up new dreams. Dreams in which scandalous things happened to King and Andrew. A grin split his face every few minutes.

Wedge got up and pulled on his Green Bay Packer slippers and his *Star Wars* robe. He quietly slid across the bedroom floor, went downstairs, stopped in the kitchen for some cookies, and ended up in the living room. He turned on the small lamp that sat on one of the end tables. It cast a yellowish glow around the room. Wedge had to admit that this room looked classy, although he'd never let on. Three of the walls were wallpapered; the other was painted the color of butterscotch. The wallpaper had outdoor scenes with pheasants and pinecones and ferns printed on. Besides the pheasants, there was some other kind of bird on the wallpaper, peeking out from between the ferns. Wedge didn't know what kind it was. The scenes were done up in shades of brown, orange, green, and a reddish color that looked like dried blood.

Scattered around the room were five brown leather bean-bag chairs. They reminded Wedge of squashed taffy apples. Or big brown balls that let out a deep breath and collapsed here and there on the floor, exhausted.

Wedge wondered who had picked out the wall-paper and the furnishings. It couldn't have been King, he thought. He doesn't have good taste. Wedge *did*, however, credit King for choosing the large framed print of a castle that hung smack in the middle of the butterscotch wall. The castle appeared to be suspended in pink and blue cotton candy. Sickening. In Wedge's opinion, it was the one thing that ruined the atmosphere of the room. He didn't know one painting could do so much damage.

Wedge wandered from room to room and dis-covered that he really liked the house. That is, when it was without the presence of the father-and-son mop handles. It would be perfect if this place belonged to just Sally and me, Wedge thought. Better yet—Sally and me and my real dad.

King's house was much bigger than Wedge and Sally's old apartment. And it didn't smell the way the old apartment did. Mrs. Erdmann, who had lived on the floor below them, always fried liver or fish and the odor wafted up through the vents. It even seemed to seep through the carpet. Also, Wedge was now spared the sight of Sally's de-coupage plaques of the Morton Salt Girl. Sally had a whole set of them, plus matching Morton Salt Girl mugs she filled with dried flowers and placed around the apartment, even on the back of the toilet. "I don't like her watching me in there," Wedge told Sally. He'd turn the mug around so the girl faced the wall. On some of the plaques and mugs the girl was old-fashioned looking; on the others, she was progressively more modern. "There's something about that little girl with her big umbrella that tugs at my heart," Sally would say. Now they sat in a box in the hall closet. Thank goodness, Wedge thought.

Wedge got a few more cookies and went back to the living room. He arranged himself comfortably in the center of the largest bean-bag chair.

He did some more figuring on his big idea. It was going to be great. Better than great.

Wedge's idea was simple and beautiful. Clean and smooth. He was going to pretend that he was sick all day long, so that when Sally called again at night and was told of his condition, she'd drive home immediately, putting a quick end to her vacation.

Wedge was quite accomplished in the area of faked illnesses. He knew all the tricks. More than once he had fooled Sally into letting him stay home from school. Most recently, he had convinced Sally that he had had the flu so he could avoid a geography test that he had forgotten to study for. The test was on the capitals of all fifty states. Wedge was only certain of Wisconsin and Illinois. He would have gotten an *F* for sure. So he heated the thermometer, groaned a lot, and mixed a concoction of cottage cheese, Parmesan cheese, Thousand Island dressing, and water. He dumped the concoction on the kitchen floor and knelt by it, holding his stomach when Sally came in for her morning tea. As usual, Sally was in a rush to make it to work without being too late and didn't have time to see through Wedge's trick. She let him stay home from school. "I'll call you from work, honey," Sally said, dropping two children's aspirins into his hand. "It's probably just a little bug."

So Wedge moved the portable TV into his room and spent the day in bed with Oreos, ice cream, Doritos, and his geography book. He ended up with a *B +* on the makeup test the next day.

Sally was easy to fool on the mornings that she worked early. Wedge hoped King was just as gullible.

Wedge finally drifted to sleep in the bean-bag chair. And that's exactly where King found him when he came downstairs for breakfast.

The voice was gentle. "Wedge? Wake up." The voice was oddly familiar, too, but Wedge couldn't quite place it. It always took him a few minutes in the morning to reestablish who and where he was. His eyes seemed like they had a film covering them; his head felt as if it were wrapped in gauze.

A hand landed on his shoulder and shook him softly. The voice again: "Wedge? Come on, son."

Hearing the word "son" affected Wedge the way a cold glass of water in the face would have. He instantly remembered who and where he was. He rolled over and turned toward King, clutching his stomach. "I think I'm sick," Wedge moaned.

8. In Sickness and in Health

Spending the day in bed with provisions while your mother is at work is one thing, but having someone like King around to take care of you all day is entirely another, Wedge soon learned. It was worse than really being sick.

King kept checking on Wedge, leaving him little time to sneak food up to his room. He also insisted on giving Wedge the suggested children's dosage of Pepto-Bismol, which Wedge thought should be used to *induce* stomachaches rather than to comfort them, it tasted so thick and pink and awful. And King even considered taking Wedge to Doctor Harris after one of Wedge's groaning sessions.

Wedge dreaded going to Doctor Harris. "I don't think I'm *that* sick," he said, deciding to quiet his groans a bit, realizing that there was a fine line between faking too much and faking the perfect amount. "I'm just sick enough to get Sally back," he whispered to himself.

"What?"

"Nothing. I just want to be alone," Wedge hissed, adjusting his pillow to cover some potato chip crumbs, in the hope that King hadn't spotted them. "Don't you have to get back to the golf course, anyway?"

"I'm not worried about the course, I'm worried about you. I hate to see you feeling bad."

The back of Wedge's neck prickled. Something inside him was uneased when King acted kindly toward him.

King brushed Wedge's hair off his forehead and felt for a fever. Wedge instantly became stiff.

King's thin hand was smooth and slightly cool. "Your temperature must be down. You seem better to me in that department."

That's because I held my head against the electric blanket right before you checked me earlier, stupid, Wedge thought.

"If you need anything, just let me know," King said lightly, tucking the blankets under Wedge's chin. "Remember, it's for better or worse, in sickness and in health."

"You didn't marry *me*," Wedge snapped. "I wish you didn't marry anybody."

King looked at Wedge, his eyes piercing right through him for a few long seconds. Wedge couldn't tell what the look meant. It wasn't a sad look or an angry look or a hurt look. It was a look that seemed completely void of emotion.

"Listen, Wedge—" King began firmly. But then he stopped. He shook his head and walked out of the room, slamming the door.

By lunchtime Wedge was losing interest in playing sick. He had run out of potato chips, the only piece of candy left in his emergency supply in his sock drawer was a single Lifesaver sticking to one of his dirty blue argyle socks, and from downstairs he could hear the wonderful sounds of food preparation—the refrigerator opening and closing, the electric can opener humming, silverware clinking, and pots and pans clanking. Wedge could also hear King's voice, singing along with a song on the radio. It was the first time Wedge had heard King sing. The voice was clear and steady. Full and strong. The voice almost drew Wedge down into the kitchen, but the thought of getting Sally home kept him in his bedroom. Sally. When she wasn't his main concern, she was always at least on the edges of his mind. Especially now that she was farther away from him than the library. Farther away from him than she'd ever been before. *And* with someone else's kid. A droopy little snotnose, at that.

Wedge went to his sock drawer and picked the Lifesaver off his sock. It was covered with blue fuzz. He popped the Lifesaver into his mouth anyway. The taste was a combination of stale butter rum and smelly socks. But Wedge pretended it tasted like two Big Macs, a large order of fries, and a medium Coke.

King's puttering noises in the kitchen grew louder, it seemed to Wedge. And then a warm, golden smell floated up to Wedge's room, causing his stomach to flutter and turn cartwheels. Wedge had never been so hungry. Campbell's Chicken Noodle. That's what King was fixing for lunch. Wedge could tell. He could practically taste it. He wanted some. Badly.

Wedge chewed what was left of his fuzzy Lifesaver (so much for pretending to have McDonald's) and bolted downstairs.

"Wedge!" King flicked his head around with a jerking motion. He was stirring a pot of soup on the stove. Wedge had guessed correctly—it was Campbell's Chicken Noodle. King was wearing a cream-colored apron. At first glance Wedge thought that it probably belonged to Sally, but then he had never seen Sally in an apron. Cooking was not one of her strong points. "I'm a gourmet when it comes to Tuna Helper, macaroni and cheese, and peanut butter and jelly," she would say.

"How are you feeling?" King asked, looking down at the soup.

"I think I'm good enough to eat something," Wedge answered, still in the doorway, hanging back a bit.

"That's a good sign." King sampled the soup. "Done," he said. "How about a small bowl of soup, a cracker or two, and a glass of orange juice?"

Wedge nodded.

King walked into the pantry and came out with two bowls. "I'm making *real* chicken soup for you for dinner. But until then this'll have to do."

King poured a small amount of soup into Wedge's bowl. Wedge was watching, hoping that King would fill the bowl. But he didn't. He didn't come close. The bowl wasn't even half full.

"I'll give you a choice," King said, filling his own bowl to the brim. "I can fix a tray for you to take up to your room, or you can eat here in the kitchen."

The kitchen smelled so good and was so sunny that Wedge said, "I'll stay here." Wedge also thought that by staying in the kitchen he might possibly find an opportunity to sneak some more soup.

They dined in silence. Wedge ate as slowly as he could, trying to make his soup last as long as possible. He counted to one hundred between each spoonful, swishing the soup around in his mouth. It occurred to Wedge that it was a rare thing for him to be eating a meal at a real kitchen table. Back at the apartment, they only had had a Formica counter with stools that Sally referred to as "the food bar." It also occurred to Wedge that he had eaten most of his meals alone (except school lunches). Before she married King, Sally had seldom eaten with Wedge, complaining that it was too hard for her to stick to her cottage cheese and yogurt diet while Wedge "gobbled up everything in sight." So Sally usually ended up in front of the TV while Wedge sat at the food bar by himself.

"Can I have a little more soup?" Wedge asked

in a voice that reminded him of Andrew's—tiny and squeaky.

"How's your stomach doing? We don't want to overdo it."

"It's okay," Wedge replied, rethinking his scheme. I should act well enough to eat a decent lunch and dinner, and then pretend to get sick again right before Sally's nightly phone call, he thought. That way I won't have to starve myself silly in order for my plan to work. "It's really great."

"Well, that was a quick recovery," King said, reaching for the pot of soup from the stove. He gave what was left to Wedge.

"Yeah, I really feel better. Almost perfect. Do you think we could have another can of soup? Please?"

"I suppose." King started laughing. "Maybe I should become a doctor—I sure worked wonders on you."

The food, the sunshine, and the prospect of another whole can of soup were making Wedge giddy; he found himself laughing right along with

King. "We could call you Doctor King," he said giggling.

"And you could be Wedge—the Wonder Patient."

King opened another can of chicken noodle soup and began singing as he heated it. And for a few minutes Wedge forgot who and where he was. He forgot that he hated King. He forgot that nothing ever made sense. However brief, he felt truly happy.

9. No!

Early afternoon. Wedge, feeling pleasantly full, found himself following King around the miniature golf course. There were no customers at the time. And King, donning his crown, was still in a happy state from lunch.

". . . so I had been dreaming of this course for years," King explained proudly, opening his arms and spreading them wide. "Ever since I learned about my namesake, King Arthur, and read about him, I wanted to *be* King Arthur. I wanted to

have my own kingdom. And this is it. All those
years of working two jobs paid off. I must have
drawn the first sketches of this course when I was
in grade school. . . ."

Wedge, nodded, half listening, faking enthusi-
asm. He was less than interested in King's story,
but he figured that King would be more sympa-
thetic to him later when he pretended to be sick
again if he acted as if he was caught up in King's
rambling.

King and Wedge both carried putters as they
walked. When he was speaking, King used his as
a pointer for extra emphasis; Wedge swished his
back and forth in the grass. "The castle is my
favorite," King said dreamily. "I could look at it
forever. Sometimes, if I stare at it long enough,
it's as if I'm in another time and place." He
paused, facing the castle. Wedge thought that
King was in a trance. His face was like a blank
piece of paper. A blank piece of paper dotted with
pink splotches.

"As you can see, this place makes me very
happy," King went on. "But not as happy as
being married to Sally and having you for a son

makes me." King put his arm around Wedge's shoulders. Wedge bristled. "Things have really been going well today, haven't they?" King said.

Wedge shrugged.

"I think this is a sign of all the good things ahead for us. And speaking of good things—you know, there's something *incredible* that's coming soon. I'm *so* excited. We were going to wait until we were all together again to announce it, but Sally said I could tell you if I wanted to. . . ."

Oh, no, Wedge thought, a flicker of fear shooting through him.

King was nearly jumping up and down now, his hands rippling with his voice. "Wedge, Sally's going to have a *baby!* I'm going to be a new father again! And you're going to get a new brother or sister!"

No! Wedge thought. *No!* He took his putter and ran up to the castle. He started beating the putter against the castle walls. *No! No! No!*

Knocking off the smallest tower. Chipping the gold paint. Smashing the plaster into tiny pieces that fell to the ground.

Wedge dropped the putter at his feet and began to cry. And then, without warning, he threw up. And this time he wasn't faking.

10. Person to Person

S ally was on her way home in the dark. When she had called that evening, King told her what had happened. They decided it was best that she and Andrew end their trip. While Wedge waited in his bed, he imagined what the baby would look like. A disaster. He pictured the baby being born with a crown growing on the top of its head. A sickly, little thing, all white with pink patches in the shape of tiny castles branded all over it. It would have a pointy nose, Wedge was sure. And the nose would most likely drip all the time. Wedge didn't think he could bear it. He pulled the blankets over his head and tried to force the horrible thoughts out of his mind.

After a few hours, Sally entered Wedge's room with a flurry. She was huffy and irritable. Slamming the door, clucking her tongue, pacing around, and moving about as if she were a hurricane storming through. It wasn't what Wedge had expected. He had expected sympathy and an apology. Maybe even a gift. At least an in-depth explanation of all the rotten things that were cramming in around him until there wasn't room to breathe. It definitely was not the homecoming he had hoped for.

Sally finally ended up on Wedge's bed, bouncing up and down on the edge of the mattress, fast and hard. When she talked she looked straight ahead at the wall, not at Wedge. In her hand she held a piece of the broken plaster from the castle.

"You're ten years old now—going on eleven— I really thought I could count on more from you," Sally said through her thin, red lips.

Wedge was stunned. Sally had never been so

harsh with him so quickly. Her words were sharp like a blade and Wedge felt instantly ashamed. He wanted to cry, but he knew he shouldn't. Am I being a baby? he wondered, gulping to keep his tears at bay. A big, fat baby?

It came to mind that his strongest feelings the last few days were the urges to cry and to eat. It seemed as if that was it. Nothing else. Take away those feelings and I'm empty, he thought, suddenly craving a Hostess Cupcake. A big, fat, empty blob.

Sally began tapping the piece of plaster against her thigh, the white dust that rubbed off looking like snow on her blue jeans. "This sure isn't how I had planned on starting our new life," she said. "I had such high hopes. I really wanted this little trip to work, and then to have it end so quickly. And like *this*." Sally tapped the plaster more rapidly and with rhythm, resembling a drummer. "And for you to act the way you did. You know, Andrew didn't get to go camping and he had his heart set on it. And you *still* never congratulated me. . . ." Sally paused— waiting, Wedge thought, for a congratulatory remark, which he refrained from offering.

"Maybe I was too optimistic," Sally continued. "Maybe I just had too much faith in you. Maybe I just thought you'd come through when I needed you most."

Wedge sat up in bed. "Well, maybe I never had a dad before . . . and maybe I don't know what to do with one," he said, his voice cracking like twigs in a fire, then sputtering. "And *maybe* I threw up because I would have liked to hear that I was getting a new brother or sister from *you*. *Not* from King. And *not* from Judith Mills, who told me first, but I didn't really believe her. . . ."

Wedge wondered who else Judith had told, how many people knew his mother was pregnant before he did. The thought made him smolder.

"*Judith Mills?*" Sally was facing Wedge now, her mouth twisted. "What about Judith *Mills?*"

Wedge told Sally all about his phone call to Judith. And then Sally burst into tears. Wedge was frightened. He watched Sally sob, not knowing what to do. Sally shook, dropping the plaster piece and rocking the bed. Her crying made her mascara streak down her cheeks like little black snakes.

"I'm so sorry, Wedge," Sally blurted out between sobs. "For everything. I never thought . . . I never wanted this to turn out this way. I didn't want you to hear it from a nosy, little busybody. I guess I told a couple of the ladies at the old apartment and Judith's mother let it slip. You know me when I have a secret; some people are like dead-end streets, but I'm like a freeway with exit ramps galore."

"It's okay," Wedge whispered, suddenly feeling older than Sally. As if he were *her* parent. Not the other way around.

Sally dabbed at her eyes. "And just remember, the only reason I married King is because I love him."

Wedge nodded.

"Listen," Sally said sniffling. "Let's talk. Really talk. Not mother to son, but person to person. And with complete honesty." Sally grabbed Wedge's hand and squeezed it so hard that he was reminded of Uncle Larry. In a hushed tone, then, she said, "You've never had a father. But don't forget—I've never had a husband. I'm just as

scared as you are. Maybe even more." She looked
downward. "Don't forget, I'm having a baby, too.
I was only eighteen when I had you—you'd think
that at twenty-eight I'd have outgrown being
scared, but I haven't. I'm scared of your being
unhappy. I'm scared of failing at being a wife. I'm
scared of having another baby. And I'm even
scared that I won't be able to lose the weight afterward," Sally admitted, laughing nervously.

That comment wasn't funny to Wedge. Sally
either treated him like *he* was twenty-eight, telling him things that he didn't really understand or
embarrassed him, or she treated him like he was
three or four.

And Wedge didn't go for this person-to-person
business. He just wanted to be treated like a son.
A son who was ten. Going on eleven.

Silence. For what seemed like a long time. Sally
was straightening her hair, using her hand as if it
were a comb, stroking it through her curls. "I've
never told anyone this," she said solemnly, wiping
her face. "I don't even know what made me think
of it, but I always had this dream as a little girl to

spend Sunday mornings in bed with my whole family. My mama and pa and Bonnie and even Jimmy, our old dog. I wasn't fussy, I didn't want breakfast in bed, or anything. Just all of us together. Safe and warm and close and snug. But your grandpa didn't go for things like that. Even kisses were an extravagance to him. And then when he and your grandma split up, my dream went out the window. Not that it would have happened, anyway. But, still, I always kept thinking that one day I'd know what that would feel like." Sally sighed. She worked on her hair a bit more. "Well, I guess that's enough honesty for now," she said abruptly. Then she left the room and came right back, carrying a large bag. "This is for you, honey," she said cheerfully. "I *was* thinking about you all the while I was gone, you know. I hope you like it, hon." She pinched his cheek in a playful manner.

It struck Wedge that Sally's moods were like a ball—bouncing without warning. Angry one minute, sad the next, then overboard sweet.

"Thanks, Sally," Wedge said. He opened the

bag. Inside was a stuffed Bucky Badger doll from Madison. "Thanks a lot."

"He's the mascot at the university," Sally told him.

"Yeah, I know."

"Kinda cute, isn't he?"

"Yeah," Wedge answered, biting his lower lip. It was really something for a younger kid. A baby, even. He would much rather have gotten a Bucky Badger sweatshirt like some of the kids at school wore. But at ten going on eleven, he was old enough to know that being remembered was the main thing.

It was nearly midnight when Sally went downstairs. Wedge was exhausted. He quickly fell into a deep sleep. Dreamless.

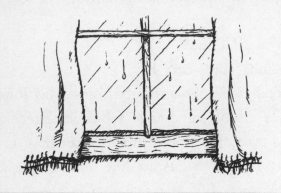

11. Stormy Weather

The next few days were punctuated by rainstorms. Mostly small showers that drizzled and stopped, drizzled and stopped, lightly dotting the leaves, grass, and flower petals. Occasionally there was a downpour with crashes of thunder and flashes of lightning. All of which meant that the golf course was closed and Wedge was held captive in the house with King, Sally, and Andrew. All day long. Day after day. For three days straight.

It occurred to Wedge that he didn't really feel

any safer now that Sally was home. He wasn't really any happier, either. His sense of relief hadn't been momentous or long-lasting. She had been gone; he had survived. It hadn't been easy, but he had done it. And something told him that it wouldn't be so hard next time.

While the rain fell Wedge did a lot of observing. Watching his family and making mental lists of all the things they did. Wedge wasn't completely certain what "normal" was. But he was sure that this wasn't it.

Most confusing to Wedge was Sally, which seemed odd since she *was* his mother. But she was changing somehow before his very eyes. Acting skittish. Or was it that he could see things differently? That she hadn't changed at all, and he had? It appeared to Wedge that Sally might cry any minute, as she had the night she came home. And all her joking and whooping seemed no more than a disguise. Wedge had felt uncomfortable when Sally had revealed so much to him in her person-to-person talk; it had stirred up things deep and silent. For the first time in his life he felt sorry for Sally. Up until then all of his pity was spent on himself.

"Are you okay?" Wedge asked Sally continuously.

"*Okay?* Wedge, I've never felt better!" she'd always answer, smiling.

On the first day of the bad weather, King tried giving Sally cooking lessons. They didn't last long. Sally kept complaining that they were dirtying too many dishes. "Why don't we just line all the pots and pans with foil, so we don't have to wash them," Sally suggested.

"Are you serious?" King asked.

Of course she was.

"I give up," King said, throwing his arms up in the air and laughing. Wedge couldn't help laughing, either. The cooking lesson ended with King and Sally playing Frisbee in the kitchen with a lid from an oleo container.

Sally called the weather number on the phone every fifteen minutes, then repeated the report to everyone in a nasal voice like the recording, even if the recording hadn't changed for hours. She also paraded around the house singing "Stormy Weather." It was a song that Wedge could only describe as screechy—at least Sally's rendition. Sally said that she thought a famous lady named Lena Horne originated the song. She pointed out that the song was *way* before her time. "Just call me Lena," she'd say before she began each time. "And Lena says we're going to have a *wonderful* life together," she'd add, holding her belly. King would frequently join in with Sally. King's voice was much better than Sally's, but she usually drowned him out. Then they did "Raindrops Keep Fallin' on My Head," King acting out the words like a game of charades as they belted away.

If this was their attempt at creating a happy home life, Wedge didn't think he was up for it.

And then there was Andrew. "We're having a baby! We're having a baby!" he squealed frequently. He lugged a box of tissues with him wherever he went. When the thunder and lightning hit, he jumped and yelped like a frightened puppy. And he spent a great portion of the day in front of the TV. He didn't just *watch* TV, he *participated* in it. And not cartoons and game shows, only public television shows.

It was most pathetic, in Wedge's opinion, when Andrew watched "Mister Rogers' Neighborhood." Like a little clone, Andrew would change from his dress shoes into his tennis shoes, and he'd even put on his cardigan sweater right along with Mr. Rogers. He'd also sing with him and snap his fingers just like Mr. Rogers did.

Mr. Rogers had always given Wedge the creeps when he was little and Sally had made him watch. Wedge also thought that Mr. Rogers snapped his fingers as if he were brain damaged. And then to see Andrew doing it the same way made Wedge cringe. If he's ever going to be my brother, Wedge thought, he'll need major reforming.

"Hey, Androop?" Wedge called one afternoon when they were alone in the family room.

"It's An-*drew!* What?"

"You know what you are?"

"What?"

"A P.T.F."

"What's *that?*" Andrew asked, looking puzzled and slightly concerned.

"It's a Public Television Freak and they're extremely abnormal," Wedge explained. "And people who are P.T.F.'s die young."

"You're lying."

"The symptoms are stringy blond hair, runny noses, and skinny bodies. Also, P.T.F.'s wear sweaters that zipper and they snap their fingers the same goofy way Mr. Rogers does."

"I don't believe you," Andrew said. "Sally told me that if you bothered me I should just ignorm you. She said that you hate that worst of all. So there," Andrew finished, crossing his arms against his tiny chest and turning his attention back to "Sesame Street." Swaying in beat with the Muppets, who were doing a jaunty musical number.

Andrew had hit a soft spot. Wedge *did* hate being ignored. And it annoyed him that Sally had told such a personal thing to Andrew. "It's ig-*nore*, not ig-*norm!*" Wedge corrected, mimicking Andrew. "You really like that junk?" Wedge persisted, making faces at the TV.

"I'm ignorming you!" Andrew shrieked, keeping his eyes glued to the Muppets.

"It's not real," Wedge said, walking up to the TV and turning the channel. "Now *this* is real." It was "General Hospital." And two people were kissing. For a long time. A very long time.

After a few more kisses, Andrew had settled back and forgotten about the Muppets. "Hey, Androop," Wedge said, getting comfortable on the floor with a pillow, "you might not be so hopeless after all."

"Shhh," Andrew hissed. "This is good."

During the last night of the rainy weather, Wedge woke up sensing something. Not something wrong. Just something different.

Wedge turned on his bedside lamp, his eyes taking a minute to adjust to the bright light. When his blinking eyes could finally focus, he saw Andrew, curled up like a cashew on the foot of his bed. He was awake. And shaking.

"You mad?" Andrew asked sheepishly.

Wedge was too groggy to answer.

"It was the thunder and lightning," Andrew explained. "And Dad and Sally's door was locked."

I'm probably too sleepy to make any sense, Wedge thought, as he patted the empty space beside him on the bed.

"Thanks, Wedge," Andrew whispered, climbing under the covers. "Thanks a lot."

"Yeah," Wedge whispered back, turning away toward the wall, wondering if it was all a dream.

12. Prince

When the rain finally stopped, Wedge felt like a freed prisoner. Just to be outside in the sunshine with the warm breeze and the insects whizzing by was a relief. So it didn't bother Wedge too much when King approached him about fixing the castle.

King cornered Wedge after breakfast. Wedge was squatting on the bottom step of the porch, sharpening a stick against a cinder block. The tip of the stick made Wedge think of the squirt tip on the top of a can of Reddi Wip. Reddi Wip used to be Wedge's favorite food. He would buy it at the Stop and Shop, a block from his old apartment building. Wedge had at least one can a week, sitting behind the apartment alone, squirting the cream onto his finger or directly into his mouth. Once, after Sally had reprimanded Wedge for snacking in bed and getting chocolate stains on his new sheets from the J. C. Penney white sale, he ate three cans of Reddi Wip to console himself. One right after the other, until he could barely move and felt like a giant marshmallow. That was the last can of Reddi Wip Wedge ever had. He vowed he'd never have another.

"Nice out, isn't it?" King asked. "A real hummer."

"Yep," Wedge replied, still sharpening the stick.

"Now that things have cleared up, you and I are going to fix the castle. We'll make it as good as new."

Since King didn't pose it as a question, Wedge didn't feel inclined to answer. He simply flung the stick into the bushes and followed King down to the shed by the course.

"You know," King said, "I apologize for the other day. I really jumped the gun and let my excitement carry me away."

"Don't mention it," Wedge said in monotone.

"I guess I wasn't thinking."

"I guess."

"I'm not sure how to say this," King said, stopping at the door to the shed, fiddling in his pockets for the key. "And I hope I'm not jumping the gun again, but I, uh . . . I love you, you know."

Sally was the only person who had said those words to Wedge before. Ever. It felt strange to hear them from someone else. But it felt oddly good, too. And something tingled inside Wedge.

"I do." King unlocked and opened the door. Inside, on the floor, were the broken pieces of the castle, a can of gold paint, and some plaster.

Wedge followed King inside. A surge of regret swept through Wedge as he scanned the objects. In a cabinet by the cash register, King rummaged for something. "Here we are," he said, grabbing a paint brush and a putty knife. He handed them to Wedge, but before Wedge could take them, King took them back. "Wait a minute," he said, glancing at his watch. "I've got an idea. Let's play a round or two of the course. We've got the time before we open. We can fix the castle later. What do you say?"

Wedge thought a minute. "I say sure."

They played three rounds of miniature golf. King won every time, but Wedge improved his score with each round. And he actually enjoyed himself. He laughed. He joked. He got excited when he had a good shot. And he completely forgot about Sally, who was sunbathing on the side of the house in a new bikini she had bought in Madison.

King helped Wedge with his stance. The proper way to grip the putter. How to hit the ball from certain angles on particular holes to avoid the obstacles. And how hard to hit it. "You've got to put a little more juice into it this time," King instructed Wedge, their first time around on the sixth hole. The cup on the sixth sat on an incline. Wedge took a deep breath and smacked the ball as hard as he could. The ball sailed into the trees way beyond the cup. "Not *that* much juice," King chuckled. Then he showed Wedge just the right amount of power to put into his swing.

When they had finished, King told Wedge that the record for the course was eight under par. "I shot it one morning last month," King said, raising and lowering his eyebrows like Groucho Marx does on the late show. "I had four holes in one."

"*Four?!*"

King nodded.

"I wish I'd get *one* hole in one."

"You will," King said. "Sally has."

Wedge felt a tinge of jealousy. "*Sally?*"

"In fact, she shot it the first time she played. It was our first date."

Wedge remembered their first date. How could he forget it? Sally had tried on about ten different outfits before she decided on one—a bright Hawaiian-print blouse and her tight jeans. She doused herself with more of her deadly lilac perfume than usual (Wedge's head swam for hours after she left). And she bought a new pair of earrings for the occasion—little, silver, dangly ones in the shape of golf clubs. "The guy I'm going out with is a golf pro, or something," she told Wedge, getting his hopes up. It was Judith Mills who ended up telling Wedge the truth—that Sally had gone out with King Simpson, the owner of Camelot. A golf pro for a potential stepfather was one thing, but a miniature golf course owner for one was entirely another, Wedge remembered thinking.

"Did Androop ever get a hole in one?" Wedge asked, hoping King would say no.

"A couple of times," King answered. "But he's played so much more than you have. And I think luck must have been on his side. You know how it is with little kids sometimes."

"Yeah."

Luck or not, getting a hole in one had suddenly lost its appeal for Wedge. Sally had gotten one. So had Andrew. It wasn't special any longer. I want something all my own, Wedge thought. Something that's just mine.

It was as if King had read Wedge's mind, because two days later Wedge *did* get something that was all his own. Something that was just his. The something was a Chesapeake Bay retriever puppy. It was the most surprised Wedge could remember being, except when Sally told him that she was going to marry King. And this was a pleasant surprise.

"Well, what do you think?" King asked Wedge, petting the puppy's wavy, brown fur. They were in the kitchen alone. Andrew was watching "Sesame Street" and Sally was back to work at the library.

"Is it a he or a she?" Wedge asked, thinking back to when he was small and was convinced that all dogs were male and all cats were female.

"A he," King said. "But what do you think?"

"I think he looks like a chocolate teddy bear."

"*And . . .*"

"And I think I love him already."

King handed the puppy to Wedge and showed him the proper way to hold him. "He's going to be a lot of work, but he'll be worth it. Oh, I should warn you, Sal wasn't too keen on the idea at first, so we have to make sure that we keep things under control—you know, toilet training and all."

Wedge's heart was skipping, he was so happy. He had never even held a puppy before, much less owned one; pets weren't allowed at his old apartment building, and no one he knew well had a dog. The puppy licked Wedge's hand, then his face. "This is great!" Wedge kept saying. "This is great!" He squeezed the puppy a bit too tightly and the puppy yelped.

"Gentle," King whispered to Wedge, smiling.

"Gentle," Wedge repeated.

"What do you think you'll name him?" King asked.

A name instantly popped into Wedge's mind. "Prince," he said. "I'm going to call him Prince."

"I can't argue with that," King said, sounding pleased.

Wedge had been worried that King and Sally would name the baby something weird—like Prince. It was a great name for a dog, but not for a human. Now they couldn't. Wedge only hoped that Sally didn't have a girl. He didn't look forward to having a baby sister named Princess.

"Why did you do this?" Wedge asked slowly, looking at Prince instead of King.

"I don't know. I just wanted to."

"Did you get something for Androop, too?"

"Nope. One puppy's enough," King said, laughing. "Andrew doesn't even know about him yet. Come on, let's go show him."

"King?" Wedge said, following King out of the kitchen. "You know the other day when I was sick up in my bed, well, I really wasn't. I was faking so Sally'd come home."

"I know."

"You *do?* You *did?*"

King nodded.

"Does Sally know?"

King shook his head no.

Prince yawned.

"Don't worry about it," King said. "I'd probably have done the same."

The stars were bright and numerous. King, Sally, Andrew, and Wedge and Prince were sitting on the porch. They were like stacked dominoes, resting against one another. Sally against King. Wedge against Sally. And Andrew against Wedge. Prince was asleep in Wedge's arms. King softly hummed a song he had heard earlier on the radio. His melody faded into the night sounds and disappeared.

"It's so clear," Sally said, looking upward, "you can see the stars twinkle. They remind me of Christmas lights. The kind that blink." She sighed deeply. "It'll be fun this Christmas—all of us can drive around at night to check out the lights in town. I'm all stirred up just thinking about it," she said, her voice sounding too loud and excited in the darkness. "*We* should do a big light display out here this Christmas! King?"

"Can we, Dad?" Andrew asked drowsily.

"I guess we could. Christmas is a long way

away, though, Sal. And lately all I can think about is the baby."

"You know me," Sally said, "I have a hard time waiting. For anything."

Waiting. It seemed to Wedge that he'd been waiting most of his life. For a father. And now he had one. But was he still waiting? Sometimes it seemed like it. Other times it didn't. He couldn't be certain. He really didn't know.

Andrew was sleeping now. Sally curled closer to King. Prince wriggled in Wedge's arms, as if trying to find a more comfortable position, crying for a moment. Wedge gently patted his head and stroked him behind his ears. Prince quieted down and settled back in the space between Wedge's arms and his chest like a small sack of warm muffins. Wedge felt needed. And very strong.

13. Practice Makes Perfect

Things were changing.

It was still summer. It was still hot. But the sun was setting earlier now. The crickets sang earlier, too. And Wedge knew that it wouldn't be long and school would begin again.

Wedge started and ended each day with at least one round of miniature golf (he had gotten three holes in one on separate occasions and his best score was six over par). Most of the time in between he spent with Prince. Prince followed

Wedge wherever he went. That is, when he wasn't gnawing on the kitchen cabinets, shredding newspapers all over the house, or doing a number on the living room carpet. If Sally got upset about the carpet, King would always say, "Practice makes perfect. And Prince is going to be perfect." Then he'd hold Prince up to Sally's face and Prince would lick her nose. That's all it took to melt Sally's heart. "I just wish you'd hurry up and be perfect," she'd say to Prince in baby talk.

Andrew was apprehensive of Prince at first. That was Wedge's fault. Once, when Andrew was watching "The Electric Company," Wedge set Prince on the rug near Andrew and then hid behind the sofa. Wedge growled and snarled, and Andrew—convinced that it was Prince—ran out of the room shrieking.

"Settle down, Androop!" Wedge shouted after him. Even though Wedge explained what had happened, Andrew still wasn't too fond of Prince.

"Why don't you just ignorm him?" Wedge said, giggling.

"I can't," Andrew replied, after blowing his

nose. "He always steals my Kleenex box and tears it up."

"I bet Mr. Rogers would like him."

"Really?"

"Oh, yes," Wedge said in his best Mr. Rogers voice. "He's soft and warm and furry and *special!*"

It took a lot of coaxing and a long time, but Andrew and Prince finally became friends. It had been a challenge; Wedge had done a good job.

They finally fixed the castle. It was an August evening and the air was cool. So cool that Wedge wore his jean jacket. King had his jean jacket on, too.

"Hey, your jacket's just like mine," King said to Wedge.

"No," Wedge said, *"your* jacket's just like *mine.*"

"I guess we're twins, huh?" King said.

They both laughed at that. They looked more like Laurel and Hardy than twins. King—tall and thin. Wedge—short and round. King was wearing his crown as usual, but Wedge hardly noticed it anymore; it just seemed a natural part of him. Wedge hardly noticed the splotches on King's face or his pointy nose, either. That's simply the way he was and Wedge was growing used to him. He couldn't imagine him any other way.

Using chicken wire and plaster, King showed Wedge how to mend the broken castle. Following King's example, Wedge tried to fasten the smallest tower back onto its base. It kept falling off.

"I can't do this," Wedge said, wiping his forehead and leaving a streak of plaster there.

"Sure you can," King assured. "Practice makes perfect."

"That's what you say to Sally about Prince."

"I think you could probably say it to anyone about anything," King said, quickly reworking the plaster while Wedge held the tower in place.

In less than an hour the castle was solid and strong and secured.

"We can paint it tomorrow," King said. "See, it *is* perfect."

"I wish I was perfect," Wedge suddenly blurted out.

"Hey," King said, "look at me." He reached down and cupped Wedge's shoulders. "Nobody's really perfect. But if anyone was—it would be you." King pulled Wedge toward him and gave him a hug.

Wedge turned stiff and cold like a statue, then, without warning, felt light and warm. King had never hugged him before. His hug was stronger than Sally's. Wedge hugged back with all his might. He didn't care if he was perfect or not.

"There's something I think I should show you," Wedge whispered to King one night before bed as King passed in the hallway. His voice was urgent.

King entered Wedge's room and Wedge locked the door behind him.

"Must be pretty important, huh?" King said.

Wedge hesitated, then pulled down his pajama pants just enough to reveal his spot. "See this?" he said quietly, keeping his eyes turned away from King. "I just wanted to show it to you in case you ever saw it and didn't know what it was. It's not some disease or anything. The doctor said it's nothing, really. I just wanted to show you, so you knew." Wedge quickly pulled his pants up, walked to the door, and unlocked it.

"I know all about spots," King said, pointing to his face, as he opened the door. "One way to look at it—they make a person unique." King turned before he left the room. "Although I'd prefer yours to mine. Yours looks like a castle."

Wedge shut the door after King. He rubbed his spot. Maybe it didn't look like Texas after all.

14. Necessary Gifts

"If you go grocery shopping with me," Sally said, "I'll take you to McDonald's for lunch."

"It's a deal!" Wedge responded. He loved McDonald's, and he didn't mind grocery shopping, either. He would have gone, McDonald's or not.

"I just don't feel like being alone today," Sally told Wedge. "I'd really love your company."

They went to the Kohl's near the interstate;

King and Andrew stayed home to man the course. Sally and Wedge each pushed their own cart. While they shopped, Wedge played a game. The object was to see how many items he could slip into other people's carts without them (or Sally) knowing. The stranger the item the better.

Wedge snuck a package of cat food into the cart of an old man while he glanced at the magazine rack. He slid a baby pacifier into the cart of a man wearing a black leather jacket with a skeleton printed on the back as the man scanned the frozen pizzas. And he dropped four cans of extra-strength deodorant into the cart of a lady who had a Chicago Cubs cap on.

Into his own cart, among other things, Wedge put some of his favorites—Cap'n Crunch, Spaghetti-O's, Doritos, and M&M's.

Being surrounded by all that food increased Wedge's hunger. He couldn't wait until they got to McDonald's. He opened the M&M's on the way.

Sally got the idea while they were eating. Wedge had ordered two Big Macs, fries, and a chocolate shake. All Sally had was decaffeinated coffee. Black. But she kept snitching Wedge's fries. "Just one," she'd say, even after her fifth and sixth fry. "I really shouldn't be eating these. I don't know what my problem is today."

"You're okay, right?" Wedge asked.

Sally sighed and grabbed another fry. "I think so. I wonder if you can get morning sickness in the afternoon."

Wedge didn't say anything. He moved what was left of his fries closer to him.

"Oh, Wedge, look at that!" Sally nearly shouted, tapping his shoulder and pointing. "Isn't that adorable?" In the back room of the restaurant a child's birthday party was in full swing. The singing had just begun—eight little kids all out of key. "I could cry," Sally said. And she did. "The birthday girl's just a button, isn't she? And look at the cake—it's got Ronald McDonald on it!"

"Yeah. It's neat, I guess. For little kids." Wedge loved the food at McDonald's, but Ronald McDonald didn't thrill him anymore. He put him in the same category as Mr. Rogers.

"I've got an idea," Sally said, drying her eyes with a napkin. "Oh, Wedge, this is going to be good. Tell me what you think."

Wedge listened.

Sally's idea was to have a party—a birthday party for the baby. The very next day. "We'll have balloons and crepe paper," Sally announced. "And I'll bake a birthday cake. One from scratch. I've only done the kind from a mix, but this is special. King can help me. Oh, Wedge, what do you think?"

Wedge hadn't seen Sally so excited in a long time. Genuinely excited. Her eyes were as big as overcoat buttons. Her hands were like butterflies, flapping and fluttering as she talked. She looked as if she might rise off the ground and float away.

"Do people do things like that?" he asked. He had never heard of it. "You said the baby won't be born until February."

"Well, people have baby showers. I don't see why we can't do this. Anyway, February's so far away. I can't wait." Sally paused. "I'll invite your Aunt Bonnie and Uncle Larry and some of the girls from work. You can invite Judith and Jackie and Eric."

"That's okay," Wedge said. "I'd rather not." He hadn't heard from them. Seeing them when school started would be soon enough.

"Let's go, honey." Sally rose from their booth. "Can you finish eating in the car? We've got a lot to do. I want to pick up the balloons and the crepe paper right away."

Driving home the plans changed.

"Maybe it would be better to keep the party just us. You know, a family affair," Sally said, her eyes fixed on the road ahead.

Wedge liked that idea for more than one reason.

"Our first, special, family celebration. Just the six of us!" Sally said with a whoop.

"Six?" Wedge said.

"Six. You and me and King and Andrew and Prince and our baby-to-be," Sally replied slowly, pumping the accelerator a bit as she said each name, for extra emphasis.

Wedge nodded his head and tightened his seat belt. "Six," he said.

At home the plans changed again.

"Do we have to get a present for the baby?" Andrew asked.

"No," King answered. "We're just having a little celebra—"

"Wait!" Sally interrupted. "That's a great idea. You can't have a party without presents. But since we don't know if the baby'll be a boy or a girl, why don't we get something for each other instead. It'll be fun."

"How about we *make* something," King suggested. "That way Andrew and Wedge won't have to empty their banks. Better yet, why don't the four of us draw names. We can each make something for *one* person—the person whose name we choose. But don't tell whose name you get. That way it'll be a surprise."

"Can we buy something if we want?" Wedge asked.

"Only if you want," King said. "You don't have to."

So they each wrote their name on a piece of paper and folded it twice. They put the paper in a bowl and one by one picked a name.

Wedge hoped for Sally. He got King.

Up in his room, Wedge tried to decide what to get King. He had one day to come up with something. He remembered when Sally was dating a guy named Bud Scapelli at Christmastime one year. Sally told Wedge that he had to get a gift for Bud even though he didn't really know (or like) him. "Just get him a necessary gift," Sally told Wedge.

"What's that?" Wedge asked, confused.

"It means, get him something he needs—like socks or underwear. Nothing special."

Wedge blushed when Sally said underwear. Socks, maybe—underwear, never.

Wedge ended up giving Bud Scapelli a free sample of men's cologne that he got at K Mart when he was doing his other shopping.

The longer he thought about the gift situation, the more confused Wedge was. He had no idea what to get King. Sally or Andrew would have been easy. For Sally you could buy anything from

suntan oil to perfume to jewelry to a box of tea
and she would love it. If he had picked Andrew,
Wedge would have bought him a couple of boxes
of man-size Kleenex.

Wedge knew he didn't want to get King a necessary gift. That was too easy. He wanted to get
him something just right for him. Whatever that
might be.

Wedge woke with a start in the middle of the
night. He was sweating. He turned on the light
and, trancelike, got out of bed and pulled the box
filled with the gifts for his real father out from
under it.

Wedge hadn't thought about the box in weeks.
But it had entered and passed through his mind as
he slept. He looked at its contents—the after-
shave, the screwdriver set, the baseball. Everything was there. But why was he looking at it in
the middle of the night? And then it dawned on
him. What he had been dreaming about. He
would give the box to King. Just as he had done
only minutes earlier in his sleep.

Wedge quietly shoved the box out to the middle of his room, turned out the light, and crawled back into bed. He closed his eyes. He knew he had made the right decision. It was necessary. It was something he needed to do.

The next afternoon Wedge wrapped the box and placed it on the floor in the corner of the kitchen. The kitchen smelled sweet and warm— of cake. Sally was racing about, tying balloons and crepe-paper streamers to all the ceiling light fixtures throughout the house. She had curlers in her hair. King had closed Camelot early and was in the basement helping Andrew finish his gift. And Prince was a wavy, brown lump snoozing near the refrigerator. Sally had tied a red bow around his neck.

"Need any help?" Wedge asked Sally.

"I don't think so, hon. I'm just about done. I have to fix my hair and then we can start."

Wedge had butterflies in his stomach. More like vultures. He couldn't wait for King to open the box. At the same time he was nervous about it. He had been saving the box for so long. Waiting for this day his entire life. He wanted everything to be perfect.

"I'll be out on the course," Wedge told Sally, wanting to be alone for a while.

"Okay, but don't be long. Remember, I've just got to do my hair."

Wedge went out and played a round of miniature golf; he knew exactly how long it took Sally to fix her hair. Surprisingly, Wedge shot his best score ever, considering his anxious feelings. Two under par. He could barely believe it. It was almost too good to be true. "Two under par!" he shouted. "I shot two under par!"

Wedge threw his putter in the air and dashed up to the house to tell everyone. He felt as if he were flying. As light as air. Because of his score. Because of the box. He turned once and looked back at the castle for a moment, then picked up speed. As he approached the porch, he could hear "Happy Birthday" already playing on the stereo. And he could see the balloons through the window, hanging down from the ceiling. They were like pieces of candy covered in bright cellophane, just waiting to be unwrapped and eaten.